praise for beautiful malady

"Ennis Rook Bashe brings us into a brief but compelling visit into a world of ghosts and machines, cybernetics, mobility and accessibility and the queer edges of the undiscovered country. These verses draw you into questions with few certain answers, histories and vantage points that need to be heard and read repeatedly. 'If I transcribed a pantheon I'd say: the god of magic is the god of death,' we're informed, and each poem moves with an assured voice and a striking imagination. This chapbook will linger with me for quite some time." — Bryan Thao Worra, former Science Fiction and Fantasy Poetry Association President (2016-2022)

"Ennis Rook Bashe fuses classic fairy-tale archetypes and imagery with new and reimagined elements rooted in the queer, disabled bodily and social experience. They balance dreams and nightmares, love and loss, old and new, life and death, in a way that feels both unique and embedded in a much longer, deeper continuity. Throughout it all, the disabled body serves as an anchor —a touchstone, a talisman—in all its beautiful, painful complexity." —Toby MacNutt, author of *If Not Skin*.

"The poems in Bashe's collection are surprising in a visceral way, delicate and sharp like a finely crafted blade flaying apathy from our observations to leave a raw, vulnerable relief in the silken textures of syllables that invite us beyond the ordinary rush of senses. *Beautiful Malady* is brutal, beatific, and irresistibly beckoning; give in to the sweet melody of its pages and listen for the fairytale of your own heart's uncertain delight." —Saba Syed Razvi, author of *In the Crocodile Gardens*

"From the melancholy to the manic, Bashe deftly uses fantasy, folklore, and pop culture to leave no corner of living with disability unexplored; weaving humor, rage, ache, and triumph into a mosaic that is utterly unique to them, yet deeply relatable." —R. Thursday

"Ennis Rook Bashe explores the painful reality of living with chronic illness and disability with gorgeous, lyrical precision. The imagery hits home with its devastating simplicity and unexpected juxtaposition, leaving the reader with bitter-sweet empathy for both the narrator and themselves." —Rebecca A. Demarest, author of *Less Than Charming*

beautiful malady

Poems

ennis rook bashe

This is a work of fiction. All of the characters, organizations, and events portrayed are either products of the author's imagination or used fictitiously.

BEAUTIFUL MALADY

Text Copyright © 2023 by Ennis Rook Bashe.

Cover art by MICHIUMS.

All rights reserved.

No part of this book may be reproduced in any form or by any electronic or mechanical means, including information storage and retrieval systems, without written permission from the author and publisher, except for the use of brief quotations in a book review.

Edited by Holly Lyn Walrath.

Published by Interstellar Flight Press

Houston, Texas.

www.interstellarflightpress.com

ISBN (eBook): 978-1-953736-23-9

ISBN (Paperback): 978-1-953736-22-2

"With profound gratitude for all my fellow writers in the disabled community and the beautiful concepts you've added to my brain-crip time, rule-bearers, collective care, access intimacy, cyborgs and tryborgs- I adore you with my whole undersized, malfunctioning heart. (Especially Liv, who makes me want to be a better writer every day.) To paraphrase San Alland as referenced in one of my favorite articles by Leah Lakshmi Piepzna-Samarasinha: we are maybe not going to save the world, but we are going to save each other."

contents

rose ghost i.	1
Theoretically, Inherited	2
On Having Had Wings	3
Seven for Beauty	4
rose ghost ii.	5
being awake for my funeral	6
my mother calls me into the living room every time there's a disabled performer on reality television	7
Mad, Without Scientist	8
rose ghost iii.	10
Ode to Illness	11
pain son	12
rose ghost iv.	13
Write What You Know	14
rose ghost v.	15
Disease Vector	17
I, Magus	18
Changelings (Migratory Legend Type 5805)	19
rose ghost vi.	21
The Blue	22
Trauma Is for People Who Fear Death	23
rose ghost vii.	25
Alternate Mode: Mobility Aid	26
this universe and all others	27
Death Is A Lesbian And She Can Pick Me Up	28
rose ghost viii.	30

Author's Note	31
Acknowledgments	35
About the Author	37
Interstellar Flight Press	39

beautiful malady

rose ghost i.

in a kingdom of midnight
where the man in the moon's face was pulled taffy
screaming and
the stars hung like knives
there was a rosebud girl whose parents could only afford
to outlive her
to reserve a catacomb for her crumbling spine
and a prince with crooked glasses always whisked away
from assassins
because shouldn't poverty be
as inevitable as winters,
shouldn't the homeless eye front doors
like diamonds,
how dare anyone succor suffering unearned?
and two sets of parents
considering miniature coffins
promising survival. wringing disinfected hands:
sweetheart I've uncovered a path to your future
won't let them condemn you to palliative waiting,
siren-humming heaven over hospital to drown you
won't let them drip poison into your meals.
blossom knotted to bramble
sword sworn to shield.

theoretically, inherited

Welcome to the country no one you love is from,
here is the grandmothers' food your intestines refuse.
No one who raised you has ever lived here.
You will have to find the way yourself.
Slow across carpeting, vertigo swirl
on hands and knees. Country of silence and shadow and
head under blankets and whisper of breath.
Country of spending more time in bed
than even the most prodigious lovers. Of lying
just so on your back.
Let's say your ancestors never cried out as much
in bed together
as you scream alone. Let's say they were married
for seventy-five years and never knew
such sensation, such ache.
To chew food with inherited mouth
for the first time in years. To map out your body and
say: look, I survived.

on having had wings

I don't like this human thing of yours; wingless,
groundbound, foot after foot. Do you like hauling
your whole solid self everywhere? Do you like
the clomp of staircases, the creak of knees?
What's it like to stand vertical as a calendar stone
with calluses growing snakeskin layers
on your heels
and sweat between your toes?
The way you have to plop your hands all over something
in order to touch it.
The way your body needs toting around
to go anywhere,
shoving into lines like conveyor belts,
thumping down steps and crashing through doors,
lugged along on boats and planes
like you're a package in the mail?
My knees don't bear my weight. That's not their job.
My body? I'm not really here, you know. I'm just
made of thoughts and glass and light.

seven for beauty

I want someone else to give my life value
like they're growing a skeleton from a knucklebone.
Stretching tendons. Coalescing meat.
The fact is I could burn with devotion
to anyone who doesn't
mind me eaten alive from the inside out.
You can have everything that twinges in me
to build an army with.
Couldn't all my agony be for something?
Something incalculable splendid
and starry white-hot. I want to be an absolute reservoir
of death-energy, a walking mausoleum,
my own beautiful tomb.
I want to be dying for, not dying of.

rose ghost ii.

in the capital of mausoleums, the dying make
the best bodyguards
wraiths a shimmer in the air behind breathing charges
senescent enchanters with single-minded focus
who would learn out-of-body projection
if their bodies were hospitable?
who would build ghost muscles
to fizzle lightbulbs if they could lift weights?
the rosegirl prepares her skin shell for leaving.
propped up on foam pillows
neck brace like a jewelry box for vertebrae
machines chugging butternut broth puree through a tube:
hello, crumbling haunted mansion of a body
in a voice like the pages of old books turning
thank you for keeping me here. thank you for letting me be
dangerous
her joints disassemble the same way her spirit
can mold itself
to slip past unseen. she kisses the forehead of her
spirit's home
takes to the air.

being awake for my funeral

I would like to play dead
in the second act of an independently produced musical.
Biting a blood capsule. Writhing as the audience goes silent, no laughs. In a musical
you can move strangely
it's called dancing. You can walk to the edge of the stage
stare at things that aren't there, wear the same outfit
every day like a second, softer skin.
No one minds if you're humming under everything.
If you are dead in the second act of a musical
all you have to do is lie there.
No wrestling with pain in choreographed tension,
no sprinting backstage tugging a sweater over a coat,
just be a strange mirror.
Waiting for the brightness around your eyes to be over.
Waiting for everyone to want to hold your hands,
gently, after the world ends,
when everyone bows.

my mother calls me into the living room every time there's a disabled performer on reality television

America you love cancer kids, before-and-after kids,
hair-grows-back, amazing-grace-I-once-was-sick.
America doesn't know what to do with kids who won't get better
won't have the decency to die and be angels
not sweet inspiration
not tragedy's gasp
America won't vote for
what scares them with mortality, the unsteady bodies theirs will someday become.
Tell us about a smiling child who recovered, they say, or
at least let his mother speak for him. At least let us
laugh.

mad, without scientist

People like me are always encouraged to go into STEM, or at least wizardry.
I don't mean
if they think you're a girl
I mean if they think you're a curse.
If you have to scrawl on the walls in blood
at least write equations. Churn out enough numbers to become a priority and thus deserve flesh.
Archetypes are invariable, nothing like dice:
you must have two hands to cradle someone else.
No mad without scientist. No scars without sneers.
The heroes are smoothed over at the end because they began complete with Strength and Constitution.
You are only allowed to limp if it's into the abyss.
At least be something to summon or unbind or pity.
At least be Always Lawful Evil, at least
subject to Greater Restoration or Remove Curse
or melting away like mist in rose-pink dawn.
I ought to live in the Monster Manual
or at least be quiet. My voice should be like
the scratch of pencils during a math test.
As biddable as clockwork.
As secret as a laboratory with scorch marks on the walls and a door behind a tapestry that no one unlocks.
Or at least I should know the alchemy
that turns flesh into gunpowder, into the promise of stardust, at least into gold.
"How do you want to do this?" is for those who rolled
well at creation.

Everyone else is either fearsome or pitiable,
either 20 or 1.

rose ghost iii.

this is how the rosegirl flicks away nightmares,
leaves her prince blinking in the constant moonlight:
hey dumbass
it is I your ghost bodyguard.
you've slept through your alarm again
the clockwork rattling a finger-bone cage,
the discordant iron bells.
if anyone tries to kill you
I will slip down their throat and whisper doom
to all their mastocytes. I will swell their throat
and make their skin writhe.
they play chess tournaments by
whispering imaginary boards
one set of footsteps in the archive stacks,
two library cards
formerly friendless
raised by tutors by nurses
the boy walking the ancestral portrait gallery writing his titles in the dust
the girl walking the ward halls holding hands
with an IV pole, making latex glove balloons
both stifling giggles when no one could find them,
hating uniforms of itchy laced brocade or identical featureless hospital gowns—
now almost all their thoughts have melded.

ode to illness

In exactly one month I will have outlived Keats
(who said life was written in water and just song
survived)
and be remarkably close to outpacing both Brontes. Letters say
Anne's deathbed flattered her.
Marianne Williamson says sickness is morbid illusion,
mental spiderweb, the "manifestation of a silent scream."
She warbled God's love drives out germs.
Can we fling illness as a failure of spirit
back to some forbidden epoch, draw forth
"all the best people are dying"
from whence it has been left to steep?
Let's say maladies are flattering.
Let's smack false prophets upside the head
with the hyphen bludgeoned into "disease" and call
lipstick arterial blood.
Sutures into diamonds. Pale bone into lace.
I can be death and absinthe and poetry, pain mingled
with sunlight,
my own nightingale and
my own tomb.

pain son

The cat and I have been hunting sunbeams.
He expects me from a throne of pillows.
He unfurls his fat belly
over the sheets.
We have been together like this in other lives and the mortar between them
blinking at each other,
afternoon, breath.
He was brought home from surgery a bleary-eyed
drunken goblin.
One leg naked like cooked turkey. Yowling in the
darkness of his cage. I told him
I understood.
The vet tech calls him a devil cat, devious, spitting fury. That no
paycheck could be worth his claws.
I hold him against my bare chest. I joke that I gave birth to him
this sprawled hairy infant with coin-gold eyes
he who inherited my pain.

rose ghost iv.

except for what hospital she lives in and which shell of organs
houses her
they know everything about each other.
let me see you, he keeps saying. let me measure my
hands against yours.
she thinks of paralyzed organs, cells digesting cells, tells
him:
run your fingers over fossil records
seek crackling manuscripts
seek decoding crossed letters, calligraphed lightless,
scratched with inkblots and tears. archaic words.
trade roads the wind travels, seek knowledge that's
twisted lives into screams,
seek fractured stars,
but don't seek me

write what you know

Here is what I know: the springwater coolness of a
needle wriggling into a vein,
the undying litany of pleasures that is
waking up sweat-soaked and then changing into clean,
dry robes.
I know porcelain and tile as pillows.
I know the spirit of my neverwoken twin sister
is whispering to me, telling me we are still on separate
paths. I know we wrapped around each other
before I had to learn the swell and flatten of lungs.
I do not know denouncement, balladry, only
the space of effort between one breath and the next.
I know that even this will end.

rose ghost v.

So there's this assassin
her bullets pry bodies open
poison more lethal than scrawling "hypochondria" across someone's life
creeping between yew trees, hollyhocks
under a brand-new-bandage moon to cull the prince
who has no idea he's in danger.
his headphones are on. he's listening to
My Favorite Demons, doodling Ars Goetia seals:
what if a raven in combat boots expounded astronomy?
the assassin's heard of an undying army
disembodied illness fakers munching Munchausen in tiny woe-is-me bites
and the royalty of coddling that enables them all
letting them waste in tilted beds
useless, unmissed.
she smells wilted roses and laughs: *don't you have a faint to feign, girl without substance?*
Get back to swooning towards your early grave.
To oversharing, underachieving, caking on new diagnoses like makeup
your soul's an all-devouring void
try me, terminal bitch.

The ghost seeps into neurons. Synapses crunch.
The assassin tries to scream,
collagen melting, chokes on her tongue and jaw,

bones shifting like a ship at sea.
my pain is a tangled electric fence. rabid bats
clinging to my hair.
pain is the fairytale stepmother forcing me to sift lentils.
a taskmaster denying life. executioner's rope.
let me give you what I know best
let me share this light with you
forbidden knowledge twisted inward.
More than electrolytes I thirst for salt in blood.

disease vector

You said I did not deserve to hold a test tube
with the same hands that held a cane
Said I did not deserve to hold a scalpel
with the same hands that shook.
As if my body's failure was my fault.
As if my existence was the infection corrupting
your data:
how dare I still live.

Do not confuse your two-hour lecture on my condition with my
postgraduate survival.
Dr. Google finds peer-reviewed journals quicker than
Dr. Assumptions,
charting fairytales
where test results were meant to go.
Pre-mortem, you ought to be proud of your work.
I am an industrial freezer because I curated my data, explained I
was dying, and they walked away.
I am a flesh tweezer because I was told that I was dying,
but not why.
I am a bone-cutting saw
supposed to be grateful for the carcass of my life.
You've made me
into the microbe that crosses the blood-brain barrier.
Into the implement that slits your throat.

i, magus

My eyes are not golden like coins or tumbled stone.
My pupils are not like a hourglass or a tiger's,
and I have never slaughtered anyone, or quaffed ale at a tavern.
I wear sweaters, not cloaks.
I can still see time.
Enough years from now, most of you will be
like my grandparents,
dragging yourselves up and down stairs
because to admit needing a cane would be
weakness, horror, loss.
Insisting on doing things for yourself.
I can get my own groceries. I can still drive.
No matter the meaningless suffering.
No matter the hours it carves out of your day.
Hourglasses weeping over grains of sand.
I see everyone wrinkled and insistent,
determined to be wrong for reasons I can't glimpse.
For so many, your body is your sword and shield.
You hoard what it can do for you.
"Only temporarily able-bodied" is a goblin to be slaughtered,
perhaps from afar with an arrow true notched,
the longbow's weight effortless in forest-honed arms. Everyone
thinks they'll be improbably lucky and die
in their sleep after decades of adventuring,
decades of strength.
If I transcribed a pantheon I'd say:
the god of magic is the god of death.

changelings (migratory legend type 5805)

According to parents mourning the living,
changelings happen when (a charm against disease
in a silver needle/the silent trolls beneath the hill)
come upon a baby who is
(untouched by God's protecting glow/ tainted
by the shudder of modern machines.)
A parent must
(boil water in an eggshell/hurl
them into a cooking fire/give
them bleach to drink like tea)
and the changeling will
(spring up laughing/call
out to its own misshapen kind/develop
normally and be as placid as a lake.)
If that fails, there are forests where wolves walk.
No breadcrumbs, no pebbles.
The changeling cannot separate lentils from ashes.
They stick a finger through the bars when you wanted
a bone.
Let's find an oven big enough to cook the whelp.
Squalling, soulless meat, they say. Let's leave it weeping in a
fallow field.

In the instant before a changeling (dies/is killed)
the faeries always come, but no one sees them.
They leave a small corpse in exchange:
this is the shell of the young soul you devoured,
something we wove from spiderwebs and moss
to satisfy teeth-gnashing hunger of your rage.

Ennis Rook Bashe

Come away, O human child
through this door is a place of rushes and soft breeze and lamb's wool where no one will hurt you
no one can zap you with the anger-magic
shooting from their shaking eyes
no one will scrape hisswhisper touch across your skin
or call you a burden heaved upon their aging back
welcome to just hearing the air sing, no furious clatter
of shouting machines
welcome to the freedom of butterflies
and friends who don't think you need to be fixed
and joy
and joy.

(Sometimes they also say:
your parents made Moloch look like
a fairy godmother/
your parents made devouring ogres look like
white bears that let you ride on their backs
/we will sing to the sparrows to peck out their
eyes/spin gold into red-hot shoes/
roll them over glass hills in a barrel of nails.
but mostly it's just:
welcome home, princes, pixies, princesses.
all our changelings, welcome home.)

rose ghost vi.

the prince kneels, headphones abandoned
pushes up his glasses and prays
to his protector-ghost:
murmur in my ear girl, rosa centifola gust girl,
your laughter like wind chimes from a fence-hidden house, life is
precarious and unexpected
let me only see your face.
coasting on victory like IV painkillers
she blurts out:
sure?
but she's swallowing fear like vitamins.
taking tinctures of doubt.

the blue

Have you got a name for the way you don't feel
anything
what's the collective noun for the parts of your body that don't
feel like yours
breathing shallow through your nose, fluorescents bright as an
alien abduction
I call mine The Blue, a wash of color at dusk
through the eyes of a deer.
through the mountain lion
calculating its trajectory of ripping out the deer's throat.
I like to play horror games because when everyone else
is on their last hit point, hiding under tables,
saying they won't go in there alone,
the Blue is an asset.
The Blue guides me to hold animatronics' bloody gears,
to speak with strangers dressed
in rags of ran-through-hell.
On a mountainside as the pine trees darken.
In a room with deep closets and no stage.
I like to play horror games. I am pretending
I am about to die.
I am pretending I am someone
who has never almost died before.

trauma is for people who fear death

My friends tell me that allergic reactions are serious
and tattoos on your ribcage hurt,
and I'm like, bold of you to think
I feel pain anymore, except I mean it.

The first time I almost died my fingers curled up
like blue-white fiddlehead ferns
when I was trying to read Jane Austen.

The second, I realized the grief I leave behind
will belong to other people.
My brain was full of resignation clouding like lint.
I waited to breathe, arose with
my parents' living room carpet swirls
embossed on my cheek.

The third time my tongue expanded onto my teeth and
the EMT joked that he was taking me to Bellevue,
which wasn't a joke.
I gave up on asking for Benadryl.
Almost more than wanting to live I wanted
New York City tap water in a recycled paper cup.
when I dragged myself to the bathroom the nurses
laughed like they'd seen a dog act at the talent show
and asked each other, why is she crawling,
what you crawling for.
My therapist told me the reason I have anxiety
is that I stereotype doctors.
He gave me a string-wrapped parcel of anecdotes
about surgeons who loved their children very much.

Ennis Rook Bashe

He said it was like a black person who stereotyped cops.
My friends tell me that not feeling fear anymore
is a reason to be frightened. On this side of fear
the world is cool blue as if seen through an icicle.
I'm standing with my toes over the edge of a diving
board and people are asking if I'm scared of the splash.
I've decided not to go to the hospital unless something needs
stitches. I won't strip for anyone in latex unless
they see where it hurts.

rose ghost vii.

and he looks at the tube that came from her intestines
and the oxygen line that went into her nose
the tape that held her shoulders together
(though sometimes her skin peeled off with it)
the stiff, heavy brace that props up her head
her compression socks and braces, the bags under her eyes
the segmented shell of stabilizers over her fingers
says:
I want to write an article citing only how your face
makes me feel.
I want to take years from my life and add them to yours.
I wish I could be the one muffling shrieks on the border
of dawn
so you could close your eyes and fall asleep.
If I can't hold back agony, let me hold you.
she didn't know that love could carve canyons in her.
that touch could stray outside for-your-own-good.
her heart monitor squealed tachycardic when they kissed
for the first time delighted: how easy it is to tug off a
hospital gown, how much skin it shows.

alternate mode: mobility aid

Every giant robot would adore
the ones who use machines to live.
How we cradle our wheelchairs after the wrecking predations of
plane crew, buff our IV fluid ports,
speak in quotes, speak in chirps.
They'd lift us with a single silver finger: you roll, too?
ah, we have fought against caste-via-construction,
against form choosing rank
bulldozers molding ourselves into guns
helicopters patching their rotary blades
disobey anyone who offers pellets of food for obedience,
who tries to swap your head with a screen of approved
conversations, your hands with stilled claws.
Or declaiming, crimson and azure and gravitas:
I have died no less than fifteen times. Locked in stasis. Orbited
dead planets. Without the past millennia of memories. Without
my face. With wires sparking from
an arm ripped off. Everything driving towards entropy deserves
to be free.

this universe and all others

Goddess of cryogenics and cave silt,
of wheelchairs on spider legs,
of clockwork hearts, sword canes in ballrooms
and bionic eyes on the spaceship bridge
one arm of translucent bone
or with an armored exoskeleton to hold in joints
goddess of wolves warning of seizures
and glowing transplant drugs extracted from corpses,
of blindness sans clairvoyance, gemstone dragon's-hoard
glass eyes
goddess of cyborgs, goddess of each wizard who leans
on their staff

Let us, in any universe,
refuse to be erased.

death is a lesbian and she can pick me up

Of course I'm dating someone.
I am utterly in love with Death.
Her abs say summer blockbuster
and her lips say this woman bites.
She comes to me with hair a shock of stoplight red
that puts all other priorities on hold.
She can fling me towards the nearest bed
from wherever I rest,
head down limbs spread eyes closed,
and I bounce on the mattress
Death says most people wouldn't have my stamina.
My adorable defiance of the inevitable. My will to
survive.

Death has a house out in the woods and a scarred chestnut horse
she speaks to softly.
A wardrobe of soft flannel shirts.
Death can hold both of my hands in one of hers,
big enough for the world. She'll bend down to kiss me
when we meet.

I feel like moaning all the time when Death touches me.
I want to dig a hole in the garden
with my bare hands and scream into it
like I'm sewing a shirt of thorns for a raven and no one
living is allowed to hear my voice.
Sooner or later we're going to move in together.
(We're long-distance right now.)
She says she'll teach me how to ballroom dance.

She says odds are I'll get good at soccer again.

What I love most about Death is that she understands
how busy I am
a tree with deep roots here, not a wilting potted plant.
Every time she beckons and I defy her
it sparks that glint in her eyes: "Clever pixie. Clever
bird. I knew you'd figure that one out."
Her voice is as low as a cello
warm and dark as buckwheat honey.
I'm her sylphide. I'm her silver fish.

Death is reliable. I trust her, though she teases me:
not yet, not yet.

rose ghost viii.

he rules remotely, remodeled his palaces into
low-income housing,
donated his ancient wealth to
those fleeing nursing homes, seeking to live
so they could pay rent in monthly checks and not cowed
obedience
because he knew what it was like to go nowhere.
and they live as ordinary secret laughing people where
day blends into night shades into day
in a cottage with rosa centifola
and a wheelchair ramp
and morning glories.
sometimes the way he touches her drowns out the pain
where she is slicker than ink, sweeter than blood
thinking, your long fingers mapping my strange velvet
skin, the parts of me that can still grip or stretch:
maybe this flesh shell is worth something on a caught
breath
when startled towards joy.
but most afternoons she leaves her frail body sleeping
and her ghost rides hospital elevators.
she descends shrieking like the winter wind
on nurses who don't sterilize for immunocompromised patients.
doctors fear her passing
and swallow back cruelty like barium: even if it makes
them gag.
she can't stand unsupported, but no one
can stand against her.

author's note

On The Concept of Alibi in Live-Action Roleplaying Theory (or: how to write an author's note when you're not good at talking about yourself)

By Ennis Rook Bashe

One of the reasons I write fiction, specifically speculative fiction, is that I don't like talking about myself. Because I don't like it, I'm not good at it. When the patient advocate asks me which doctor dislocated my shoulder, I stare at the beige wall behind her and mumble vaguely coherently. When a woman on the street runs up to me to ask about my cancer diagnosis and if we're being treated at the same hospital (she's a breast cancer patient; I shaved my head in a fit of gender three months prior), I nod through the conversation. I don't even like asking for a seat on the subway, even if it means having to sit on the floor all through Manhattan.

I'm young and I'm pretty and the average person can't pronounce my diagnosis and the average mental health professional hasn't even heard that medical trauma exists—what good could talking about myself possibly do? What would it provide, except another chance to be disbelieved?

Author's Note

One of the things I get most excited about when it comes to making a new LARP character is figuring out how disability fits into their backstory. Finch, who I played all through college at a Long Island campground turned medieval village, was used as a poison tester, murdered and revived by their usurping necromancer uncle before their current life as a feisty urchin. (What I wore to become Finch: a vest I made in costume design class, lockpicks hidden in the laces of a corset belt, my nice boots, knee braces under leggings.)

Lothenn, a green-skinned wood troll adopted by an entire human faction, was buried alive in a volcano for his kindness to mortals, and left with scars and weakness despite his immortality. (What makes Lothenn a separate person from me includes: Green Wet & Wild eyeshadow used as contour, a Legolas cosplay wig without the ears, a wooden cane from the Renaissance fair.) I'm not good at talking about myself, but I can tell you everything about my LARP characters and what's wrong with them.

The characters I'm most drawn to, whether as a player or as a fan, also tend to have trauma in their backstories. Finch flew into a hysterical rage when invited to attend her uncle's wedding to another character's mother, and Lothenn bolted into the woods in unseeing panic when forced to watch a dissident burning alive. I loved Maximum Ride and River Tam when I was a child because they were the only people I knew who'd ever been hurt by doctors. I tell every Sandman fan I know that Constantine was locked in a mental hospital after failing to save a young girl's life and having a mental breakdown about it and subjected to nonconsensual electroshock treatment.

I am good at talking about pain and fear and trauma and helplessness and more pain. Other people's, at least. I can write, for instance, that Lothenn fears anything related to fire. That he was furious with disbelief when two rocks-for-brains trolls joked about climbing inside a volcano to get warm, and made direct eye contact with them as he told them what exactly it felt like to be inside a volcano. That he coughed up cherry-flavored fake blood after the Troll King took away the magic he used to stabilize his lungs. That, afterwards, he shook with terror in a friend's arms because he thought he was dying. I can write that Constantine would rather cauterize her own wounds than risk seeing a doctor again, or that River Tam goes into a fugue state when getting her space vaccinations.

When I talk about myself—when I talk about my body in relation to myself—I try to skirt the edges of the truth. Some of it is because I can't remember, certain events leaving big blank spaces punctuated by oddly vivid sense-impressions. Some of it is because putting the bad things into words tends to set off my heart rate issues. I have also gotten very good at not talking about myself because people hate it when I do. I think these are universal trauma reactions, but also universal chronically ill experiences.

When the people most prone to hurting you have life-and-death power over you, whether they are offering medical help or are just community members with the ability to take away your social capital and leave you without a safety net, honesty is dangerous. Speaking as yourself, about what's happened to you, punctures egos and leads to accusations of whining or malingering. It leads to more pain.

My people swap guides on what to say to get doctors to run tests, how to keep the emergency room from deeming an arterial dissection or stomach paralysis psychosomatic, how to convince your home health aide to put on a mask to reduce the odds of getting a potentially fatal virus. "Don't describe how your pain feels—describe the chores and work it prevents you from doing."

Author's Note

"Say your symptoms are bothering someone else, especially if that someone else is a man." We know what words and phrases are off-limits if we want to survive.

In the LARP community, we have a concept called alibi. I'm going to attempt to distill years of Nordic theory monographs as concisely as I can: basically, alibi means that you are not your character, even though your character might just be you in a bad wig. If your character tortures someone else's character, you can go for drinks afterwards. If you're shy in real life, you can play a character who threatens to pistol-whip anyone who gets on your bad side. You have an alibi and don't have to stick to your real-world persona.

Similarly, I view speculative fiction as a way for marginalized people to share what has been silenced. The unspeakable things. The things we spend years learning not to speak about because we lose friends and alienate people if we do.

This is a poetry book about wizards, scientists, robots, necromancers, and changelings.

It is a book of alibis.

acknowledgments

Disease Vector appeared in Marías at Sampaguitas.

I read "The Blue" and "Trauma Is For People Who Fear Death" at Taboo Adieu, an event presented by Strange Bird Theatre Company.

about the author

Ennis Rook Bashe is a queer romance novelist and poet whose work has appeared in *Strange Horizons, Cricket*, and *Liminality Magazine.* Their debut chapbook, *Glitter Blood*, was an Elgin Award nominee. If you enjoyed the disability-related themes in this chapbook, you may also enjoy their fantasy romance series *Hunters of the Cairn,* set in a world where only disabled and chronically ill people can become monster hunters. Find more Ennis at https://linktr.ee/ennisrookbashe.

- twitter.com/rookthebird
- instagram.com/ennisrookbashe
- tiktok.com/@rookthebird
- amazon.com/Ennis-Rook-Bashe

interstellar flight press

Interstellar Flight Press is an indie speculative publishing house. We feature innovative works from the best new writers in science fiction and fantasy. In the words of Ursula K. Le Guin, we need "writers who can see alternatives to how we live now, can see through our fear-stricken society and its obsessive technologies to other ways of being, and even imagine real grounds for hope."

Find us online at www.interstellarflightpress.com.

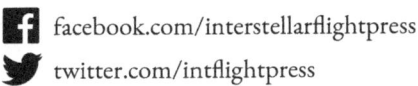

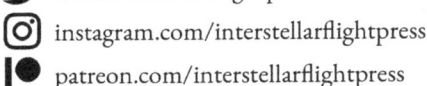

facebook.com/interstellarflightpress
twitter.com/intflightpress
instagram.com/interstellarflightpress
patreon.com/interstellarflightpress

CPSIA information can be obtained
at www.ICGtesting.com
Printed in the USA
BVHW041951180523
664437BV00002B/41

9 781953 736222